MYRON'S MAGIC COW

To Michael Austin, wherever he is, who brought
Myron to life on the stage of Trinity Elementary School.
And to all the children in my charge in
all my years of teaching – M. N.

For my lovely wife, Alex – J.

Barefoot Books
2067 Massachusetts Ave
Cambridge, MA 02140

This book has been printed on 100% acid-free paper
The illustrations were prepared digitally, using a mixture
of scanned, painted, drawn and photographed sources
Design by Louise Millar, London
Typeset in Aunt Mildred
Color separation by Grafiscan, Verona
Printed and bound in Singapore
by Tien Wah Press Pte Ltd

Library of Congress Cataloging-in-Publication Data
Newman, Marlene.
Myron / written by Marlene Newman ; illustrated by Jago.
p. cm.
Summary: While performing his most despised chore--running to the store for his
mother--Myron acquires a magical cow and makes a special wish.
ISBN 1-84148-496-2 (hardcover : alk. paper) [1. Cows--Fiction. 2. Wishes--Fiction.
3. Humorous stories.] I. Jago, ill. II. Title.

PZ7.N4843My 2005
[E]--dc22

2004028590

1 3 5 7 9 8 6 4 2

Acknowledgments
I would like to acknowledge the people who have supported my efforts and given me
most valuable criticism. They include Candace Whitman, Rolaine Hochstein,
Deyva Arthur, Jody and Cecilia MacDonald, Nancy Lynk, Sue Miller, Eric Luper
and all the members of the Capital District Society of Children's Book Writers
and Illustrators, and, of course, my loving family – M. N.

MYRON'S MAGIC COW

written by Marlene Newman

illustrated by Jago

Barefoot Books
Celebrating Art and Story

Whenever Mama needed something, Will was too busy and Rita was too little to help. So it was always Myron who was sent to the store.

Like last Sunday morning, when Mama decided to make pancakes for breakfast. She got her bowl, spoon, measuring cup and griddle. She took out flour, eggs and the carton of milk ... but the milk was all gone.

"I need milk for the pancakes!" she called.
"Myron, take a five out of my pocketbook and run
down to the store."

And so, as usual, Myron had to go. Out of the
apartment, down the hall, into the elevator,
through the lobby and up the busy street he went.

"Psst!" Myron heard a peculiar sound.

"Psst!"

There it was again. Myron turned the corner. Once more he heard an insistent "psst" from the alley that separated two tall buildings.

He looked over his shoulder and saw a girl with curly blond hair holding a rope.

"Hey," the girl whispered. "I hear there's no milk at your house."

Myron knew not to talk to strangers, and this was no one he knew. How could she know they were out of milk?

"Hey," the girl repeated. "I've got something for you. You'll never have to go to the store for milk again."

She tugged at the rope, and dragged a huge cow out of the alley and on to the street.

"What do you think of her?" she asked. "A dopey guy who said his name was Jack just traded her with me. I gave him a pack of moldy old beans and he gave me the cow. Not a bad deal, hey?"

Now Myron had seen pictures of cows in books and on cartoons, on TV and in movies. But he had never ever before been face-to-face with a real-live-honest-to-goodness cow. He was speechless.

"Listen," the girl continued, "there are already three bears in my car and the cow just won't fit. You need milk and I need money — so let's cut a deal. How much cash do you have on you?"

Myron pinched himself to see if he was awake. Then he opened his hand and looked at the wrinkled bill.

"Myron, this is your lucky day. That's exactly how much the cow will cost you," the girl said. She snatched the bill out of Myron's palm and handed him the rope.

Before Myron could say yes, no or maybe, the girl jumped into the back of the car. The bear at the wheel revved the engine and they vanished down the street in a cloud of smelly black smoke.

Myron wondered what Mama would say — what Mama would do when he returned home with this extremely large container of milk. Well, at least it would be better than no milk at all. Myron looked at the cow. The cow looked at Myron. Neither was particularly happy to be at an opposite end of the same rope.

People on the street were beginning to stare. Some whispered, others laughed. And still others shouted insults.

Myron tugged at the rope. The cow plopped down on the sidewalk and made a loud, unpleasant noise.

"Look at the weird kid with the cow," someone cried. And Myron cried, too.

He grabbed the rope with both hands and pulled really, really hard. This time, the cow stood up and Myron sat down — with a hard bump.

He got to his feet and pulled again. The cow moved.
Myron pulled again. The cow came closer. Myron took a
step. So did the cow. Myron walked up the street. The cow
followed. They walked past the supermarket, the bakery,
the video store, the playground and the school.

Myron tried to act as if it were perfectly normal to be pulling a cow along the street on a Sunday morning.

And so, pushing and pulling, stopping and starting, they struggled down the street until they reached Myron's building.

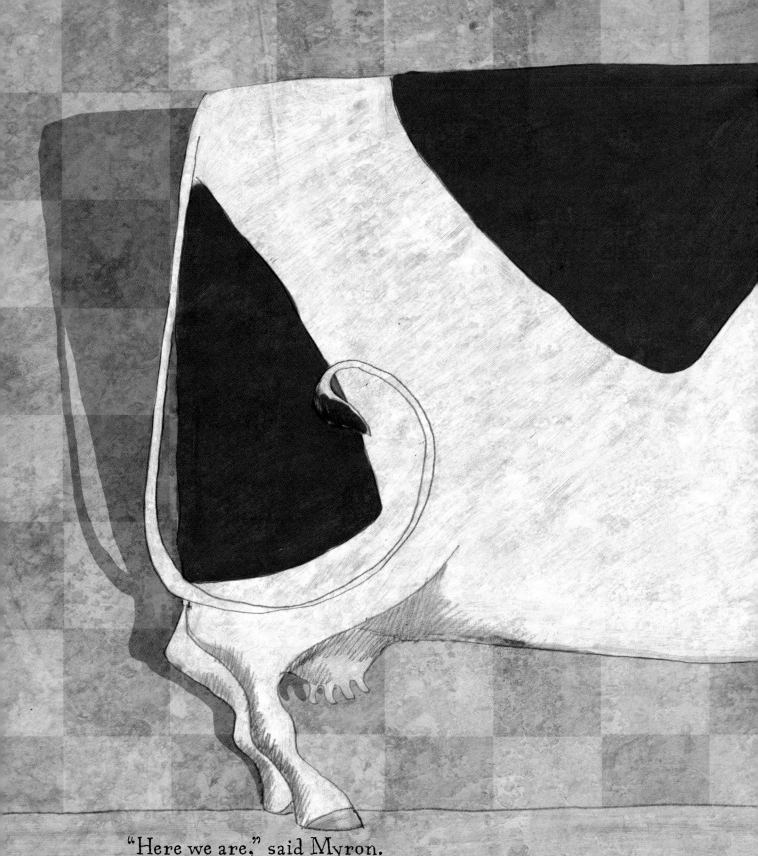

"Here we are," said Myron.

The cow nodded and followed him inside. Myron pressed
the buzzer to get into the elevator, but nothing happened.

"Open sesame!" said the cow, and the door swung open.
Myron spun around in astonishment, and the cow gave
him a nudge. "Hurry up, or it will shut again."

"I don't understand."

"What don't you understand? Open sesame?"

Myron understood the words. He just couldn't believe where they were coming from. "Excuse me," he said. "I didn't know cows could talk."

"Don't let it get around. We've always been able to talk. But as long as no one knows, we get to hear all kinds of things. I've been around, you know, and I've picked up a few tricks here and there. Learned that one from my old pal Ali Baba. What's your floor?"

The elevator rattled up to the fifth floor. Myron still didn't know what to tell Mama. The door slid open. Myron pulled the rope. The cow wouldn't budge. A little light flashed on. Myron got behind the cow and shoved her out just as the elevator door closed behind them.

He started down the long hall, pulling and tugging at
his end of the rope as the cow pulled and tugged at hers.
Still pulling and pushing, Myron fumbled with his key
and opened the door.

"Myron," Mama called. "Is that you? Did you get milk?"

"Sort of," Myron mumbled.

"What? I can't hear you. How many times have I told you to open your mouth and speak clearly? Where's the milk? I can't make pancakes without milk. Myron ... come on ... it's almost lunchtime and we haven't had breakfast."

"I'm coming," Myron answered. But he was hunting through the toy chest for his pail and shovel.

"If I can get enough milk for the pancakes," he thought, "I'll have time to figure out what to tell Mama."

"Myron ... I'm waiting. What's the matter? Can't you bring the milk in here?"

"I'll be there in a minute, Mama."

Myron found the plastic pail. He put it under the cow and began to squeeze and pull and squeeze and pull.

Nothing happened. He squeezed and pulled and squeezed again. Still nothing happened. He was close to tears. He stood up and looked the cow right in the eye.

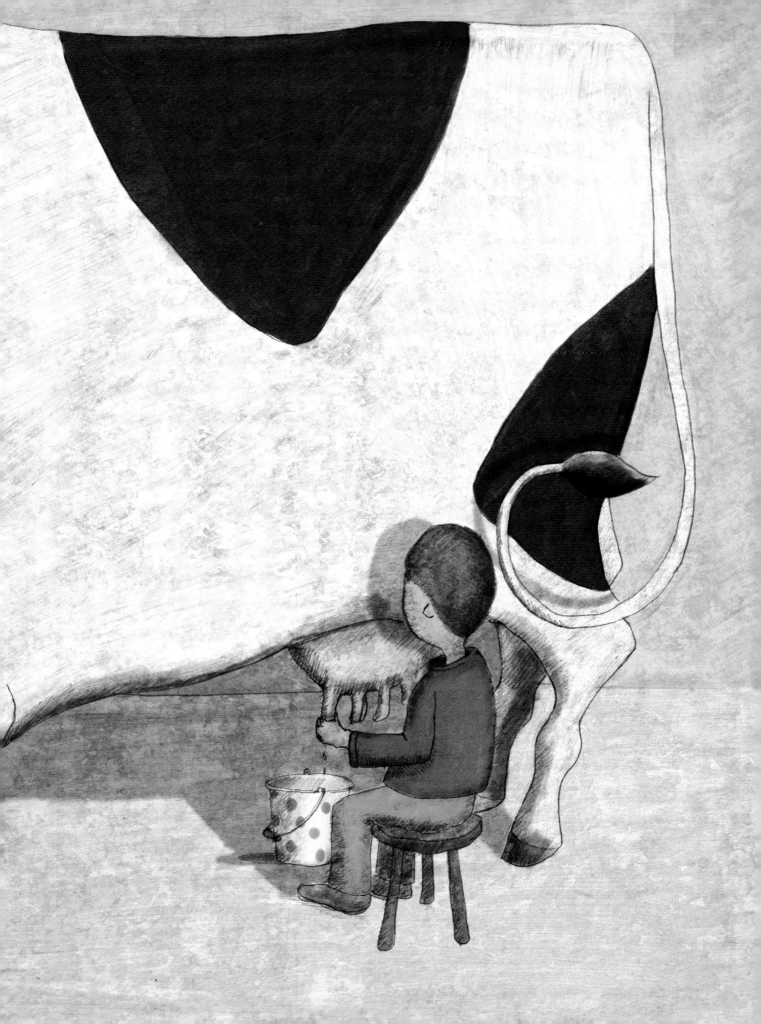

"Listen," he said to her. "I'm sorry about this, but I'm not happy either. I wish you would cooperate. Maybe I'll figure a way out of this for both of us. Please..."

"Since you put it that way."

"What?"

"The magic word."

"What?"

"You know ... the magic word – *please* – the magic word."

"I don't understand."

"Which word don't you understand? Magic? Please?"

"Both — I mean neither — I mean please — could you help me out here?"

The cow gave a superior smile.

"You humans are all the same. You have no idea what we animals can do. Still, at least you helped me get away from that awful girl. Never trust blondes, that's what I say, especially when they're girls traveling with bears. Who knows what they might have done to me if you hadn't walked by. I owe you one, kid. What'll you have — regular, skim or one percent?"

"Whatever," Myron answered, too flustered to decide.

He squeezed again and his plastic pail filled with fresh, creamy milk.

"Thank you," he said as he raced into the kitchen.

The cow was looking around the apartment when Myron returned with the empty pail.

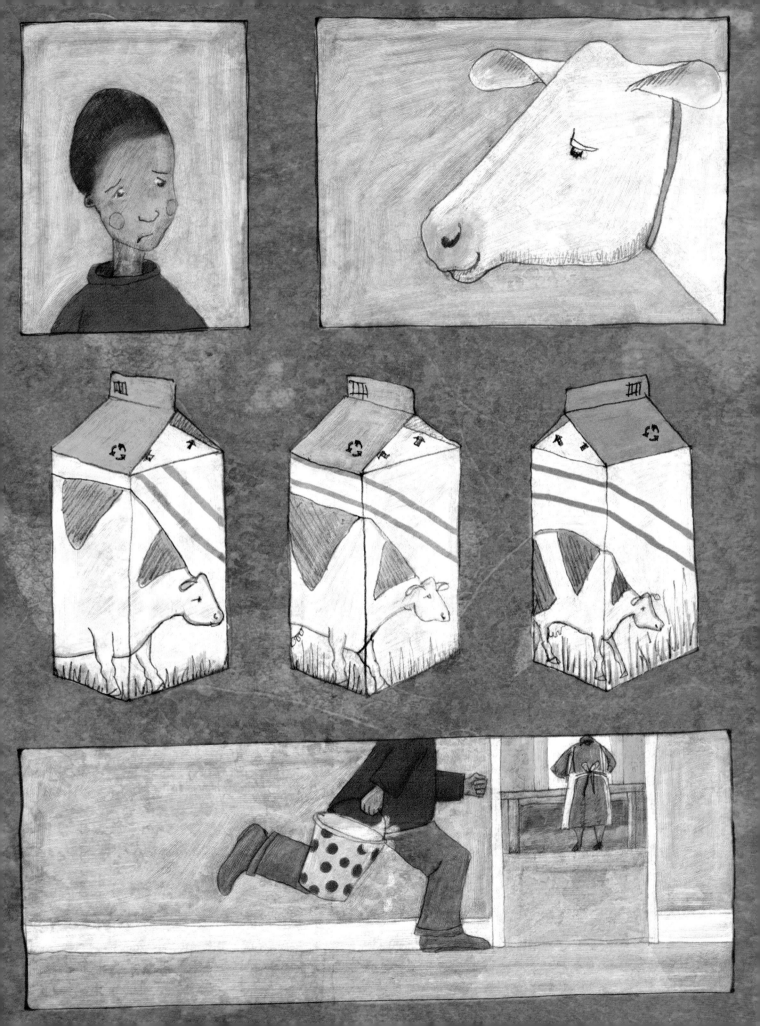

"That should do it for now," he said. "But I still don't know how to explain this to my mom."

"Look, kid," the cow replied. "I don't just give milk. I can do some other stuff, too."

"Like what?"

"Ever hear of genies?"

"You mean..."

"Yeah, that's exactly what I mean."

"Do I get three wishes?"

"You used one already. Remember ... the milk?"

"I'd better be careful. Let me think. I wish I wasn't so nervous. I'd be able to think better."

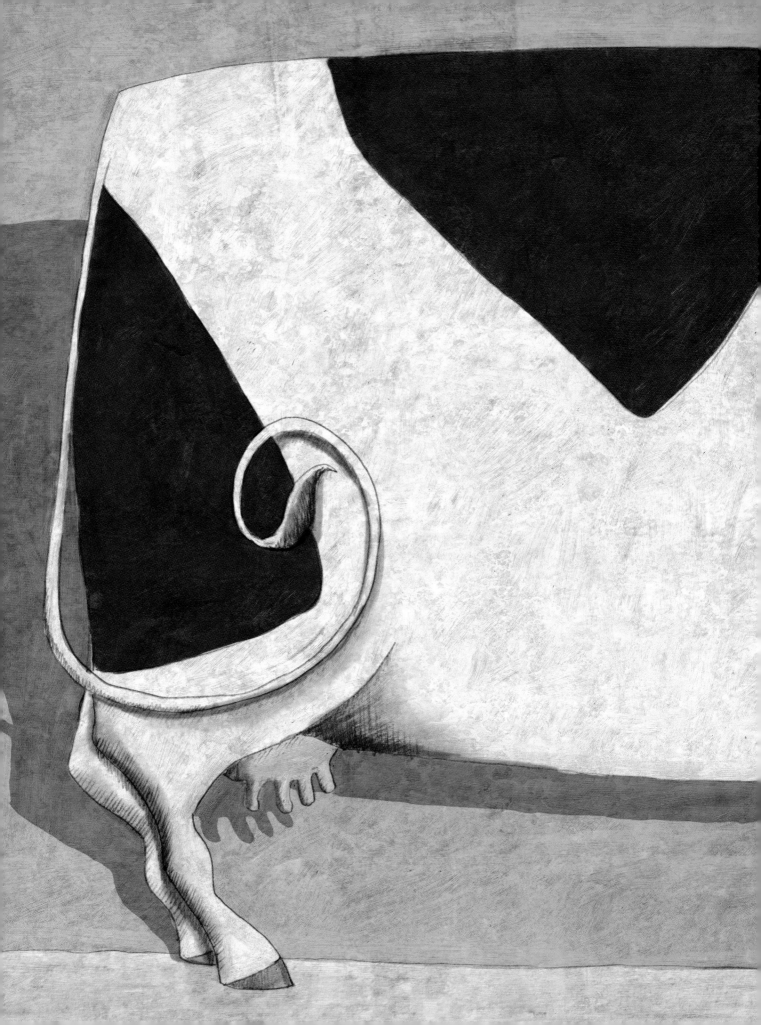

And a calm he had never before felt came over Myron as the cow said, "Two! One more to go." Myron could think clearly now. He was certain he would make a wise wish. He put his arms around the cow and said, "I wish someone else would have to go to the store once in a while."

A great flash of light filled the room and when it had passed, the cow was gone.

Mama called from the kitchen, "Pancakes will be ready soon. Will, go to the store for syrup. And pick up another carton of eggs while you're there."

Myron sighed a long, happy sigh and smiled all the way down to the tips of his toes.

Then he looked down at the floor — was that an egg?

He'd never seen such a big egg in his life.

It was shiny, too. Could it be ... a golden egg?

Barefoot Books
Celebrating Art and Story

At Barefoot Books, we celebrate art and story with books that open the hearts and minds of children from all walks of life, inspiring them to read deeper, search further, and explore their own creative gifts. Taking our inspiration from many different cultures, we focus on themes that encourage independence of spirit, enthusiasm for learning, and acceptance of other traditions. Thoughtfully prepared by writers, artists and storytellers from all over the world, our products combine the best of the present with the best of the past to educate our children as the caretakers of tomorrow.

www.barefootbooks.com